War and Peace

BOOK THIRTEEN : 1812

By Leo Tolstoy

Double 9 BOOKS

War and Peace Book 13
by Leo Tolstoy

ISBN: 978-93-94973-61-9

Published by

DOUBLE 9 BOOKS
2/13-B, Ansari Road
Daryaganj, New Delhi - 110002
info@double9books.com
www.double9books.com
Tel. 011-40042856

Printed in India.

About the Author

Leo Tolstoy was a Russian creator known for his books War and Peace which is viewed as the best book of pragmatist fiction. Tolstoy is additionally viewed as world's best author by quite a few people. Additionally an ethical scholar and a social reformer, Tolstoy had extreme moralistic points of view. In later life, he turned into an intense Christian rebel and anarcho-conservative.

Leo Tolstoy Born in Yasnaya Polyana on September 9, 1828, He had a place with a notable honorable Russian family. He was the fourth among five offspring of Count Nikolai Ilyich Tolstoy and Countess Mariya Tolstaya, both of whom kicked the bucket passing on their youngsters to be raised by family members.

In 1844, Tolstoy was acknowledged into Kazan University. Incapable to graduate past the subsequent year, Tolstoy got back to Yasnava Polyana and afterward invested energy going among Moscow and St. Petersburg. With some functioning information on a few dialects, he turned into a multilingual. Yet again the recently observed youth pulled in Tolstoy towards drinking, visiting massage parlors and most betting which left him in weighty obligation and anguish however Tolstoy before long acknowledged he was carrying on with a brutish life and endeavored college tests with the expectation that he would acquire a situation with the public authority, yet finished yet up in Caucuses serving in the military continuing in the strides of his senior sibling.

In Year 1862, Leo Tolstoy wedded Sophia Andreevna Behrs, generally called Sonya, who was 16 years more youthful than him. The couple had thirteen youngsters, of which, five passed on at an early age. Sonya went about as Tolstoy's secretary, editor and monetary chief while he made two out of his most prominent works. Their initial wedded life was loaded up with happiness.

He started composing his show-stopper, War and Peace in 1862. The six volumes of the work were distributed somewhere in the range of 1863 and 1869. With 580 characters got from history and others made by Tolstoy, this extraordinary novel takes on investigating the hypothesis of history and the irrelevance of noted figures like Alexander and Napoleon. Anna Karenina, Tolstoy's next epic was begun in 1873 and distributed totally in 1878.

Contents

BOOK THIRTEEN : 1812

CHAPTER I

Man's mind cannot grasp the causes of events in their completeness, but the desire to find those causes is implanted in man's soul. And without considering the multiplicity and complexity of the conditions any one of which taken separately may seem to be the cause, he snatches at the first approximation to a cause that seems to him intelligible and says: "This is the cause!" In historical events (where the actions of men are the subject of observation) the first and most primitive approximation to present itself was the will of the gods and, after that, the will of those who stood in the most prominent position—the heroes of history. But we need only penetrate to the essence of any historic event—which lies in the activity of the general mass of men who take part in it—to be convinced that the will of the historic hero does not control the actions of the mass but is itself continually controlled. It may seem to be a matter of indifference whether we understand the meaning of historical events this way or that; yet there is the same difference between a man who says that the people of the West moved on the East because Napoleon wished it and a man who says that this happened because it had to happen, as there is between those who declared that the earth was stationary and that the planets moved round it and those who admitted that they did not know what upheld the earth, but knew there were laws directing its movement and that of the other planets. There is, and can be, no cause of an historical event except the one cause of all causes. But there are laws directing events, and some of these laws are known to us while we are conscious of others we cannot comprehend. The discovery of these laws is only possible when we have quite abandoned the attempt to find the cause in the will of some one man, just as the discovery of the laws of the motion of the planets was possible only when men abandoned the conception of the fixity of the earth.

The historians consider that, next to the battle of Borodinó and the occupation of Moscow by the enemy and its destruction by fire, the most important episode of the war of 1812 was the movement of the Russian army from the Ryazána to the Kalúga road and to the Tarútino camp—the so-called flank march across the KrásnayaPakhrá River. They ascribe the glory of that achievement of genius to different men and dispute as to whom the honor is due. Even foreign historians, including the French, acknowledge the genius of the Russian commanders when they speak of that flank march. But it is hard to understand why military writers, and following them others, consider this flank march to be the profound conception of some one man who saved Russia and destroyed Napoleon. In the first place it is hard to understand where the profundity and genius of this movement lay, for not much mental effort was needed to see that the best position for an army when it is not being attacked is where there are most provisions; and even a dull boy of thirteen could have guessed that the best position for an army after its retreat from Moscow in 1812 was on the Kalúga road. So it is impossible to understand by what reasoning the historians reach the conclusion that this maneuver was a profound one. And it is even more difficult to understand just why they think that this maneuver was calculated to save Russia and destroy the French; for this flank march, had it been preceded, accompanied, or followed by other circumstances, might have proved ruinous to the Russians and salutary for the French. If the position of the Russian army really began to improve from the time of that march, it does not at all follow that the march was the cause of it.

That flank march might not only have failed to give any advantage to the Russian army, but might in other circumstances have led to its destruction. What would have happened had Moscow not burned down? If Murat had not lost sight of the Russians? If Napoleon had not remained inactive? If the Russian army at KrásnayaPakhrá had given battle as Bennigsen and Barclay advised? What would have happened had the French attacked the Russians while they were marching beyond the Pakhrá? What would have happened if on approaching Tarútino, Napoleon had attacked the Russians with but a tenth of the energy he had shown when he attacked them at Smolénsk? What would have happened had the French moved on Petersburg?... In any of these eventualities the flank march that brought salvation might have proved disastrous.

The third and most incomprehensible thing is that people studying history deliberately avoid seeing that this flank march cannot be attributed to any one man, that no one ever foresaw it, and that in reality, like the retreat from Filí, it did not suggest itself to anyone in its entirety, but resulted—moment by moment, step by step, event by event—from an endless number of most diverse circumstances and was only seen in its entirety when it had been accomplished and belonged to the past.

At the council at Filí the prevailing thought in the minds of the Russian commanders was the one naturally suggesting itself, namely, a direct retreat by the Nízhni road. In proof of this there is the fact that the majority of the council voted for such a retreat, and above all there is the well-known conversation after the council, between the commander in chief and Lanskóy, who was in charge of the commissariat department. Lanskóy informed the commander in chief that the army supplies were for the most part stored along the Oká in the Túla and Ryazán provinces, and that if they retreated on Nízhni the army would be separated from its supplies by the broad river Oká, which cannot be crossed early in winter. This was the first indication of the necessity of deviating from what had previously seemed the most natural course—a direct retreat on Nízhni-Nóvgorod. The army turned more to the south, along the Ryazán road and nearer to its supplies. Subsequently the inactivity of the French (who even lost sight of the Russian army), concern for the safety of the arsenal at Túla, and especially the advantages of drawing nearer to its supplies caused the army to turn still further south to the Túla road. Having crossed over, by a forced march, to the Túla road beyond the Pakhrá, the Russian commanders intended to remain at Podólsk and had no thought of the Tarútino position; but innumerable circumstances and the reappearance of French troops who had for a time lost touch with the Russians, and projects of giving battle, and above all the abundance of provisions in Kalúga province, obliged our army to turn still more to the south and to cross from the Túla to the Kalúga road and go to Tarútino, which was between the roads along which those supplies lay. Just as it is impossible to say when it was decided to abandon Moscow, so it is impossible to say precisely when, or by whom, it was decided to move to Tarútino. Only when the army had got there, as the result of innumerable and varying forces, did people begin to assure themselves that they had desired this movement and long ago foreseen its result.

CHAPTER II

The famous flank movement merely consisted in this: after the advance of the French had ceased, the Russian army, which had been continually retreating straight back from the invaders, deviated from that direct course and, not finding itself pursued, was naturally drawn toward the district where supplies were abundant.

If instead of imagining to ourselves commanders of genius leading the Russian army, we picture that army without any leaders, it could not have done anything but make a return movement toward Moscow, describing an arc in the direction where most provisions were to be found and where the country was richest.

That movement from the Nízhni to the Ryazán, Túla, and Kalúga roads was so natural that even the Russian marauders moved in that direction, and demands were sent from Petersburg for Kutúzov to take his army that way. At TarútinoKutúzov received what was almost a reprimand from the Emperor for having moved his army along the Ryazán road, and the Emperor's letter indicated to him the very position he had already occupied near Kalúga.

Having rolled like a ball in the direction of the impetus given by the whole campaign and by the battle of Borodinó, the Russian army—when the strength of that impetus was exhausted and no fresh push was received—assumed the position natural to it.

Kutúzov's merit lay, not in any strategic maneuver of genius, as it is called, but in the fact that he alone understood the significance of what had happened. He alone then understood the meaning of the French army's inactivity, he alone continued to assert that the battle of Borodinó had been a victory, he alone—who as commander in chief might have been expected to be eager to attack—employed his whole strength to restrain the Russian army from useless engagements.

The beast wounded at Borodinó was lying where the fleeing hunter had left him; but whether he was still alive, whether he was strong and merely lying low, the hunter did not know. Suddenly the beast was heard to moan.

The moan of that wounded beast (the French army) which betrayed its calamitous condition was the sending of Lauriston to Kutúzov's camp with overtures for peace.

Napoleon, with his usual assurance that whatever entered his head was right, wrote to Kutúzov the first words that occurred to him, though they were meaningless.

MONSIEUR LE PRINCE KOUTOUZOV: I am sending one of my adjutants-general to discuss several interesting questions with you. I beg your Highness to credit what he says to you, *especially when he expresses the sentiment of esteem and special regard I have long entertained for your person. This letter having no other object, I pray God, monsieur le prince Koutouzov, to keep you in His holy and gracious protection!*

NAPOLEON

MOSCOW, OCTOBER 30, 1812

Kutúzov replied: "I should be cursed by posterity were I looked on as the initiator of a settlement of any sort. *Such is the present spirit of my nation.*" But he continued to exert all his powers to restrain his troops from attacking.

During the month that the French troops were pillaging in Moscow and the Russian troops were quietly encamped at Tarútino, a change had taken place in the relative strength of the two armies—both in spirit and in number—as a result of which the superiority had passed to the Russian side. Though the condition and numbers of the French army were unknown to the Russians, as soon as that change occurred the need of attacking at once showed itself by countless signs. These signs were: Lauriston's mission; the abundance of provisions at Tarútino; the reports coming in from all sides of the inactivity and disorder of the French; the flow of recruits to our regiments; the fine weather; the long rest the Russian soldiers had enjoyed, and the impatience to do what they had been assembled for, which usually shows itself in an army that has been resting; curiosity as to what the French army, so long lost sight of, was doing; the boldness with which our outposts now scouted close up to the French stationed at Tarútino; the news of easy successes gained by peasants and guerrilla troops over the French, the envy aroused by this; the desire for revenge that lay in the heart of every Russian as long as the French were in Moscow, and (above all) a dim consciousness in every soldier's mind that the relative strength of the armies had changed and that the advantage was now on our side. There was a substantial change in the relative strength, and an advance had become inevitable. And at once, as a clock begins to strike and chime as soon as the minute hand has completed a full circle, this change was shown by an increased activity, whirring, and chiming in the higher spheres.

CHAPTER III

The Russian army was commanded by Kutúzov and his staff, and also by the Emperor from Petersburg. Before the news of the abandonment of Moscow had been received in Petersburg, a detailed plan of the whole campaign had been drawn up and sent to Kutúzov for his guidance. Though this plan had been drawn up on the supposition that Moscow was still in our hands, it was approved by the staff and accepted as a basis for action. Kutúzov only replied that movements arranged from a distance were always difficult to execute. So fresh instructions were sent for the solution of difficulties that might be encountered, as well as fresh people who were to watch Kutúzov's actions and report upon them.

Besides this, the whole staff of the Russian army was now reorganized. The posts left vacant by Bagratión, who had been killed, and by Barclay, who had gone away in dudgeon, had to be filled. Very serious consideration was given to the question whether it would be better to put A in B's place and B in D's, or on the contrary to put D in A's place, and so on—as if anything more than A's or B's satisfaction depended on this.

As a result of the hostility between Kutúzov and Bennigsen, his Chief of Staff, the presence of confidential representatives of the Emperor, and these transfers, a more than usually complicated play of parties was going on among the staff of the army. A was undermining B, D was undermining C, and so on in all possible combinations and permutations. In all these plottings the subject of intrigue was generally the conduct of the war, which all these men believed they were directing; but this affair of the war went on independently of them, as it had to go: that is, never in the way people devised, but flowing always from the essential attitude of the masses. Only in the highest spheres did all these schemes, crossings, and interminglings appear to be a true reflection of what had to happen.

Prince Michael Ilariónovich! (wrote the Emperor on the second of October in a letter that reached Kutúzov after the battle at Tarútino) Since September 2 Moscow has been in the hands of the enemy. Your last reports were written on the twentieth, and during all this time not only has no action been taken against the enemy or for the relief of the ancient capital, but according to your last report you have even retreated farther. Sérpukhov is already occupied by an enemy detachment and Túla with its famous arsenal, so indispensable to the army, is in danger. From General Wintzingerode's reports, I see that an enemy corps of ten thousand men is moving on the Petersburg road. Another corps of several thousand men is moving on Dmítrov. A third has advanced along the Vladímir road, and a fourth, rather considerable detachment is stationed between Rúza and Mozháysk. Napoleon himself was in Moscow as late as the twenty-fifth. In view of all this information, when the enemy has scattered his forces in large detachments, and with Napoleon and his Guards in Moscow, is it possible that the enemy's forces confronting you are so considerable as not to allow of your taking the offensive? On the contrary, he is probably pursuing you with detachments, or at most with an army corps much weaker than the army entrusted to you. It would seem that, availing yourself of these circumstances, you might advantageously attack a weaker one and annihilate him, or at least oblige him to retreat, retaining in our hands an important part of the provinces now occupied by the enemy, and thereby averting danger from Túla and other towns in the interior. You will be responsible if the enemy is able to direct a force of any size against Petersburg to threaten this capital in which it has not been possible to retain many troops; for with the army entrusted to you, and acting with resolution and energy, you have ample means to avert this fresh calamity. Remember that you have still to answer to our offended country for the loss of Moscow. You have experienced my readiness to reward you. That readiness will not weaken in me, but I and Russia have a right to expect from you all the zeal, firmness, and success which your intellect, military talent, and the courage of the troops you command justify us in expecting.

But by the time this letter, which proved that the real relation of the forces had already made itself felt in Petersburg, was dispatched, Kutúzov had found himself unable any longer to restrain the army he commanded from attacking and a battle had taken place.

On the second of October a Cossack, Shapoválov, who was out scouting, killed one hare and wounded another. Following the wounded hare he made his way far into the forest and came upon the left flank of Murat's army, encamped there without any precautions. The Cossack laughingly told his comrades how he had almost fallen into the hands of the French. A cornet, hearing the story, informed his commander.

The Cossack was sent for and questioned. The Cossack officers wished to take advantage of this chance to capture some horses, but one of the superior officers, who was acquainted with the higher authorities, reported the incident to a general on the staff. The state of things on the staff had of late been exceedingly strained. Ermólov had been to see Bennigsen a few days previously and had entreated him to use his influence with the commander in chief to induce him to take the offensive.

"If I did not know you I should think you did not want what you are asking for. I need only advise anything and his Highness is sure to do the opposite," replied Bennigsen.

The Cossack's report, confirmed by horse patrols who were sent out, was the final proof that events had matured. The tightly coiled spring was released, the clock began to whirr and the chimes to play. Despite all his supposed power, his intellect, his experience, and his knowledge of men, Kutúzov—having taken into consideration the Cossack's report, a note from Bennigsen who sent personal reports to the Emperor, the wishes he supposed the Emperor to hold, and the fact that all the generals expressed the same wish—could no longer check the inevitable movement, and gave the order to do what he regarded as useless and harmful—gave his approval, that is, to the accomplished fact.

CHAPTER IV

Bennigsen's note and the Cossack's information that the left flank of the French was unguarded were merely final indications that it was necessary to order an attack, and it was fixed for the fifth of October.

On the morning of the fourth of October Kutúzov signed the dispositions. Toll read them to Ermólov, asking him to attend to the further arrangements.

"All right—all right. I haven't time just now," replied Ermólov, and left the hut.

The dispositions drawn up by Toll were very good. As in the Austerlitz dispositions, it was written—though not in German this time:

"The First Column will march here and here," "the Second Column will march there and there," and so on; and on paper, all these columns arrived at their places at the appointed time and destroyed the enemy. Everything had been admirably thought out as is usual in dispositions, and as is always the case, not a single column reached its place at the appointed time.

When the necessary number of copies of the dispositions had been prepared, an officer was summoned and sent to deliver them to Ermólov to deal with. A young officer of the Horse Guards, Kutúzov's orderly, pleased at the importance of the mission entrusted to him, went to Ermólov's quarters.

"Gone away," said Ermólov's orderly.

The officer of the Horse Guards went to a general with whom Ermólov was often to be found.

"No, and the general's out too."

The officer, mounting his horse, rode off to someone else.

"No, he's gone out."

"If only they don't make me responsible for this delay! What a nuisance it is!" thought the officer, and he rode round the whole camp. One man said he had seen Ermólov ride past with some other generals, others said he must have returned home. The officer searched till six o'clock in the evening without even stopping to eat. Ermólov was nowhere to be found and no one knew where he was. The officer snatched a little food at a comrade's, and rode again to the vanguard to find Milorádovich. Milorádovich too was away, but here he was told that he had gone to a ball at General Kíkin's and that Ermólov was probably there too.

"But where is it?"

"Why, there, over at Échkino," said a Cossack officer, pointing to a country house in the far distance.

"What, outside our line?"

"They've put two regiments as outposts, and they're having such a spree there, it's awful! Two bands and three sets of singers!"

The officer rode out beyond our lines to Échkino. While still at a distance he heard as he rode the merry sounds of a soldier's dance song proceeding from the house.

"In the meadows... in the meadows!" he heard, accompanied by whistling and the sound of a *torban*, drowned every now and then by shouts. These sounds made his spirits rise, but at the same time he was afraid that he would be blamed for not having executed sooner the important order entrusted to him. It was already past eight o'clock. He dismounted and went up into the porch of a large country house which had remained intact between the Russian and French forces. In the refreshment room and the hall, footmen were bustling about with wine and viands. Groups of singers stood outside the windows. The officer was admitted and immediately saw all the chief generals of the army together, and among them Ermólov's big imposing figure. They all had their coats unbuttoned and were standing in a semicircle with flushed and animated faces, laughing loudly. In the middle of the room a short handsome general with a red face was dancing the *trepák* with much spirit and agility.

"Ha, ha, ha! Bravo, Nicholas Iványch! Ha, ha, ha!"

The officer felt that by arriving with important orders at such a moment he was doubly to blame, and he would have preferred to wait; but one of the generals espied him and, hearing what he had come about, informed Ermólov.

Ermólov came forward with a frown on his face and, hearing what the officer had to say, took the papers from him without a word.

"You think he went off just by chance?" said a comrade, who was on the staff that evening, to the officer of the Horse Guards, referring to Ermólov. "It was a trick. It was done on purpose to get Konovnítsyn into trouble. You'll see what a mess there'll be tomorrow."

CHAPTER V

Next day the decrepit Kutúzov, having given orders to be called early, said his prayers, dressed, and, with an unpleasant consciousness of having to direct a battle he did not approve of, got into his *calèche* and drove from Letashóvka (a village three and a half miles from Tarútino) to the place where the attacking columns were to meet. He sat in the *calèche*, dozing and waking up by turns, and listening for any sound of firing on the right as an indication that the action had begun. But all was still quiet. A damp dull autumn morning was just dawning. On approaching TarútinoKutúzov noticed cavalrymen leading their horses to water across the road along which he was driving. Kutúzov looked at them searchingly, stopped his carriage, and inquired what regiment they belonged to. They belonged to a column that should have been far in front and in ambush long before then. "It may be a mistake," thought the old commander in chief. But a little further on he saw infantry regiments with their arms piled and the soldiers, only partly dressed, eating their rye porridge and carrying fuel. He sent for an officer. The officer reported that no order to advance had been received.

"How! Not rec..." Kutúzov began, but checked himself immediately and sent for a senior officer. Getting out of his *calèche*, he waited with drooping head and breathing heavily, pacing silently up and down. When Eýkhen, the officer of the general staff whom he had summoned, appeared, Kutúzov went purple in the face, not because that officer was to blame for the mistake, but because he was an object of sufficient importance for him to vent his wrath on. Trembling and panting the old man fell into that state of fury in which he sometimes used to roll on the ground, and he fell upon Eýkhen, threatening him with his hands, shouting and loading him with gross abuse. Another man, Captain Brózin, who happened to turn up and who was not at all to blame, suffered the same fate.

"What sort of another blackguard are you? I'll have you shot! Scoundrels!" yelled Kutúzov in a hoarse voice, waving his arms and reeling.

He was suffering physically. He, the commander in chief, a Serene Highness who everybody said possessed powers such as no man had ever had in Russia, to be placed in this position—made the laughingstock of the whole army! "I needn't have been in such a hurry to pray about today, or have kept awake thinking everything over all night," thought he to himself. "When I was a chit of an officer no one would have dared to mock me so... and now!" He was in a state of physical suffering as if from corporal punishment, and could not avoid expressing it by cries of anger and distress. But his strength soon began to fail him, and looking about him, conscious of having said much that was amiss, he again got into his *calèche* and drove back in silence.

His wrath, once expended, did not return, and blinking feebly he listened to excuses and self-justifications (Ermólov did not come to see him till the next day) and to the insistence of Bennigsen, Konovnítsyn, and Toll that the movement that had miscarried should be executed next day. And once more Kutúzov had to consent.

CHAPTER VI

Next day the troops assembled in their appointed places in the evening and advanced during the night. It was an autumn night with dark purple clouds, but no rain. The ground was damp but not muddy, and the troops advanced noiselessly, only occasionally a jingling of the artillery could be faintly heard. The men were forbidden to talk out loud, to smoke their pipes, or to strike a light, and they tried to prevent their horses neighing. The secrecy of the undertaking heightened its charm and they marched gaily. Some columns, supposing they had reached their destination, halted, piled arms, and settled down on the cold ground, but the majority marched all night and arrived at places where they evidently should not have been.

Only Count Orlóv-Denísov with his Cossacks (the least important detachment of all) got to his appointed place at the right time. This detachment halted at the outskirts of a forest, on the path leading from the village of Stromílova to Dmítrovsk.

Toward dawn, Count Orlóv-Denísov, who had dozed off, was awakened by a deserter from the French army being brought to him. This was a Polish sergeant of Poniatowski'scorps, who explained in Polish that he had come over because he had been slighted in the service: that he ought long ago to have been made an officer, that he was braver than any of them, and so he had left them and wished to pay them out. He said that Murat was spending the night less than a mile from where they were, and that if they would let him have a convoy of a hundred men he would capture him alive. Count Orlóv-Denísov consulted his fellow officers.

The offer was too tempting to be refused. Everyone volunteered to go and everybody advised making the attempt. After much disputing and arguing, Major-General Grékov with two Cossack regiments decided to go with the Polish sergeant.

"Now, remember," said Count Orlóv-Denísov to the sergeant at parting, "if you have been lying I'll have you hanged like a dog; but if it's true you shall have a hundred gold pieces!"

Without replying, the sergeant, with a resolute air, mounted and rode away with Grékov whose men had quickly assembled. They disappeared into the forest, and Count Orlóv-Denísov, having seen Grékov off, returned, shivering from the freshness of the early dawn and excited by what he had undertaken on his own responsibility, and began looking at the enemy camp, now just visible in the deceptive light of dawn and the dying campfires. Our columns ought to have begun to appear on an open declivity to his right. He looked in that direction, but though the columns would have been visible quite far off, they were not to be seen. It seemed to the count that things were beginning to stir in the French camp, and his keen-sighted adjutant confirmed this.

"Oh, it is really too late," said Count Orlóv, looking at the camp.

As often happens when someone we have trusted is no longer before our eyes, it suddenly seemed quite clear and obvious to him that the sergeant was an impostor, that he had lied, and that the whole Russian attack would be ruined by the absence of those two regiments, which he would lead away heaven only knew where. How could one capture a commander in chief from among such a mass of troops!

"I am sure that rascal was lying," said the count.

"They can still be called back," said one of his suite, who like Count Orlóv felt distrustful of the adventure when he looked at the enemy's camp.

"Eh? Really... what do you think? Should we let them go on or not?"

"Will you have them fetched back?"

"Fetch them back, fetch them back!" said Count Orlóv with sudden determination, looking at his watch. "It will be too late. It is quite light."

And the adjutant galloped through the forest after Grékov. When Grékov returned, Count Orlóv-Denísov, excited both by the abandoned attempt and by vainly awaiting the infantry columns that still did not appear, as well as by the proximity of the enemy, resolved to advance. All his men felt the same excitement.

"Mount!" he commanded in a whisper. The men took their places and crossed themselves.... "Forward, with God's aid!"

"Hurrah-ah-ah!" reverberated in the forest, and the Cossack companies, trailing their lances and advancing one after another as if poured out of a sack, dashed gaily across the brook toward the camp.

One desperate, frightened yell from the first French soldier who saw the Cossacks, and all who were in the camp, undressed and only just waking up, ran off in all directions, abandoning cannons, muskets, and horses.

Had the Cossacks pursued the French, without heeding what was behind and around them, they would have captured Murat and everything there. That was what the officers desired. But it was impossible to make the Cossacks budge when once they had got booty and prisoners. None of them listened to orders. Fifteen hundred prisoners and thirty-eight guns were taken on the spot, besides standards and (what seemed most important to the Cossacks) horses, saddles, horsecloths, and the like. All this had to be dealt with, the prisoners and guns secured, the booty divided—not without some shouting and even a little fighting among themselves—and it was on this that the Cossacks all busied themselves.

The French, not being farther pursued, began to recover themselves: they formed into detachments and began firing. Orlóv-Denísov, still waiting for the other columns to arrive, advanced no further.

Meantime, according to the dispositions which said that "the First Column will march" and so on, the infantry of the belated columns, commanded by Bennigsen and directed by Toll, had started in due order and, as always happens, had got somewhere, but not to their appointed places. As always happens the men, starting cheerfully, began to halt; murmurs were heard, there was a sense of confusion, and finally a backward movement. Adjutants and generals galloped about, shouted, grew angry, quarreled, said they had come quite wrong and were late, gave vent to a little abuse, and at last gave it all up and went forward, simply to get somewhere. "We shall get somewhere or other!" And they did indeed get somewhere, though not to their right places; a few eventually even got to their right place, but too late to be of any use and only in time to be fired at. Toll, who in this battle played the part of Weyrother at Austerlitz, galloped assiduously from place to place, finding everything upside down everywhere. Thus he stumbled on Bagovút's corps in a wood when it was already broad daylight, though the corps should long before have joined Orlóv-Denísov. Excited and vexed by the failure and supposing that someone must be responsible for it, Toll galloped up to the commander of the corps and began upbraiding him severely, saying that he ought to be shot. General Bagovút, a fighting old soldier of placid temperament, being also upset by all the delay, confusion, and cross-purposes, fell into a rage to everybody's surprise and quite contrary to his usual character and said disagreeable things to Toll.

"I prefer not to take lessons from anyone, but I can die with my men as well as anybody," he said, and advanced with a single division.

Coming out onto a field under the enemy's fire, this brave general went straight ahead, leading his men under fire, without considering in his agitation whether going into action now, with a single division, would be of any use or no. Danger, cannon balls, and bullets were just what he needed in his angry mood. One of the first bullets killed him, and other bullets killed many of his men. And his division remained under fire for some time quite uselessly.

CHAPTER VII

Meanwhile another column was to have attacked the French from the front, but Kutúzov accompanied that column. He well knew that nothing but confusion would come of this battle undertaken against his will, and as far as was in his power held the troops back. He did not advance.

He rode silently on his small gray horse, indolently answering suggestions that they should attack.

"The word *attack* is always on your tongue, but you don't see that we are unable to execute complicated maneuvers," said he to Milorádovich who asked permission to advance.

"We couldn't take Murat prisoner this morning or get to the place in time, and nothing can be done now!" he replied to someone else.

When Kutúzov was informed that at the French rear—where according to the reports of the Cossacks there had previously been nobody—there were now two battalions of Poles, he gave a sidelong glance at Ermólov who was behind him and to whom he had not spoken since the previous day.

"You see! They are asking to attack and making plans of all kinds, but as soon as one gets to business nothing is ready, and the enemy, forewarned, takes measures accordingly."

Ermólov screwed up his eyes and smiled faintly on hearing these words. He understood that for him the storm had blown over, and that Kutúzov would content himself with that hint.

"He's having a little fun at my expense," said Ermólov softly, nudging with his knee Raévski who was at his side.

Soon after this, Ermólov moved up to Kutúzov and respectfully remarked:

"It is not too late yet, your Highness—the enemy has not gone away—if you were to order an attack! If not, the Guards will not so much as see a little smoke."

Kutúzov did not reply, but when they reported to him that Murat's troops were in retreat he ordered an advance, though at every hundred paces he halted for three quarters of an hour.

The whole battle consisted in what Orlóv-Denísov's Cossacks had done: the rest of the army merely lost some hundreds of men uselessly.

In consequence of this battle Kutúzov received a diamond decoration, and Bennigsen some diamonds and a hundred thousand rubles, others also received pleasant recognitions corresponding to their various grades, and following the battle fresh changes were made in the staff.

"That's how everything is done with us, all topsy-turvy!" said the Russian officers and generals after the Tarútino battle, letting it be understood that some fool there is doing things all wrong but that we ourselves should not have done so, just as people speak today. But people who talk like that either do not know what they are talking about or deliberately deceive themselves. No battle—Tarútino, Borodinó, or Austerlitz—takes place as those who planned it anticipated. That is an essential condition.

A countless number of free forces (for nowhere is man freer than during a battle, where it is a question of life and death) influence the course taken by the fight, and that course never can be known in advance and never coincides with the direction of any one force.

If many simultaneously and variously directed forces act on a given body, the direction of its motion cannot coincide with any one of those forces, but will always be a mean—what in mechanics is represented by the diagonal of a parallelogram of forces.

If in the descriptions given by historians, especially French ones, we find their wars and battles carried out in accordance with previously formed plans, the only conclusion to be drawn is that those descriptions are false.

The battle of Tarútino obviously did not attain the aim Toll had in view—to lead the troops into action in the order prescribed by the dispositions; nor that which Count Orlóv-Denísov may have had in view—to take Murat prisoner; nor the result of immediately destroying the whole corps, which Bennigsen and others may have had in view; nor the aim of the officer who wished to go into action to distinguish himself; nor that of the Cossack who wanted more booty than he got, and so on. But if the aim of the battle was what actually resulted and what all the Russians of that day desired—to drive the French out of Russia and destroy their army—it is quite clear that the battle of Tarútino, just because of its incongruities, was exactly what was wanted at that stage of the campaign. It would be difficult and even impossible to imagine any result more opportune than the actual outcome of this battle. With a minimum of effort and insignificant losses, despite the greatest confusion, the most important results of the whole campaign were attained: the transition from retreat to advance, an exposure of the weakness of the French, and the administration of that shock which Napoleon's army had only awaited to begin its flight.

CHAPTER VIII

Napoleon enters Moscow after the brilliant victory *de la Moskowa*; there can be no doubt about the victory for the battlefield remains in the hands of the French. The Russians retreat and abandon their ancient capital. Moscow, abounding in provisions, arms, munitions, and incalculable wealth, is in Napoleon's hands. The Russian army, only half the strength of the French, does not make a single attempt to attack for a whole month. Napoleon's position is most brilliant. He can either fall on the Russian army with double its strength and destroy it; negotiate an advantageous peace, or in case of a refusal make a menacing move on Petersburg, or even, in the case of a reverse, return to Smolénsk or Vílna; or remain in Moscow; in short, no special genius would seem to be required to retain the brilliant position the French held at that time. For that, only very simple and easy steps were necessary: not to allow the troops to loot, to prepare winter clothing—of which there was sufficient in Moscow for the whole army—and methodically to collect the provisions, of which (according to the French historians) there were enough in Moscow to supply the whole army for six months. Yet Napoleon, that greatest of all geniuses, who the historians declare had control of the army, took none of these steps.

He not merely did nothing of the kind, but on the contrary he used his power to select the most foolish and ruinous of all the courses open to him. Of all that Napoleon might have done: wintering in Moscow, advancing on Petersburg or on Nízhni-Nóvgorod, or retiring by a more northerly or more southerly route (say by the road Kutúzov afterwards took), nothing more stupid or disastrous can be imagined than what he actually did. He remained in Moscow till October, letting the troops plunder the city; then, hesitating whether to leave a garrison behind him, he quitted Moscow, approached Kutúzov without joining battle, turned to the right and reached Málo-Yaroslávets, again without attempting to break through and take the road Kutúzov took, but retiring instead to Mozháysk along the devastated Smolénsk road. Nothing more stupid than that could have been devised, or more disastrous for the army, as the sequel showed. Had Napoleon's aim been to destroy his army, the most skillful strategist could hardly have devised any series of actions that would so completely have accomplished that purpose, independently of anything the Russian army might do.

Napoleon, the man of genius, did this! But to say that he destroyed his army because he wished to, or because he was very stupid, would be as unjust as to say that he had brought his troops to Moscow because he wished to and because he was very clever and a genius.

In both cases his personal activity, having no more force than the personal activity of any soldier, merely coincided with the laws that guided the event.

The historians quite falsely represent Napoleon's faculties as having weakened in Moscow, and do so only because the results did not justify his actions. He employed all his ability and strength to do the best he could for himself and his army, as he had done previously and as he did subsequently in 1813. His activity at that time was no less astounding than it was in Egypt, in Italy, in Austria, and in Prussia. We do not know for certain in how far his genius was genuine in Egypt—where forty centuries looked down upon his grandeur—for his great exploits there are all told us by Frenchmen. We cannot accurately estimate his genius in Austria or Prussia, for we have to draw our information from French or German sources, and the incomprehensible surrender of whole corps without fighting and of fortresses without a siege must incline Germans to recognize his genius as the only explanation of the war carried on in Germany.

But we, thank God, have no need to recognize his genius in order to hide our shame. We have paid for the right to look at the matter plainly and simply, and we will not abandon that right.

His activity in Moscow was as amazing and as full of genius as elsewhere. Order after order and plan after plan were issued by him from the time he entered Moscow till the time he left it. The absence of citizens and of a deputation, and even the burning of Moscow, did not disconcert him. He did not lose sight either of the welfare of his army or of the doings of the enemy, or of the welfare of the people of Russia, or of the direction of affairs in Paris, or of diplomatic considerations concerning the terms of the anticipated peace.

CHAPTER IX

With regard to military matters, Napoleon immediately on his entry into Moscow gave General Sabastiani strict orders to observe the movements of the Russian army, sent army corps out along the different roads, and charged Murat to find Kutúzov. Then he gave careful directions about the fortification of the Krémlin, and drew up a brilliant plan for a future campaign over the whole map of Russia.

With regard to diplomatic questions, Napoleon summoned Captain Yákovlev, who had been robbed and was in rags and did not know how to get out of Moscow, minutely explained to him his whole policy and his magnanimity, and having written a letter to the Emperor Alexander in which he considered it his duty to inform his Friend and Brother that Rostopchín had managed affairs badly in Moscow, he dispatched Yákovlev to Petersburg.

Having similarly explained his views and his magnanimity to Tutólmin, he dispatched that old man also to Petersburg to negotiate.

With regard to legal matters, immediately after the fires he gave orders to find and execute the incendiaries. And the scoundrel Rostopchín was punished by an order to burn down his houses.

With regard to administrative matters, Moscow was granted a constitution. A municipality was established and the following announcement issued:

INHABITANTS OF MOSCOW!

Your misfortunes are cruel, but His Majesty the Emperor and King desires to arrest their course. Terrible examples have taught you how he punishes disobedience and crime. Strict measures have been taken to put an end to disorder and to re-establish public security. A paternal administration, chosen from among yourselves, will form your municipality or city government. It will take care of you, of your needs, and of your welfare. Its members will be distinguished by a red ribbon worn across the shoulder, and the mayor of the city will wear a white belt as well. But when not on duty they will only wear a red ribbon round the left arm.

The city police is established on its former footing, and better order already prevails in consequence of its activity. The government has appointed two commissaries general, or chiefs of police, and twenty commissaries or captains of wards have been appointed to the different wards of the city. You will recognize them by the white ribbon they will wear on the left arm. Several churches of different denominations are open, and divine service is performed in them unhindered. Your fellow citizens are returning every day to their homes and orders have been given that they should find in them the help and protection due to their misfortunes. These are the measures the government has adopted to re-establish order and relieve your condition. But to achieve this aim it is necessary that you should add your efforts and should, if possible, forget the misfortunes you have suffered, should entertain the hope of a less cruel fate, should be certain that inevitable and ignominious death awaits those who make any attempt on your persons or on what remains of your property, and finally that you should not doubt that these will be safeguarded, since such is the will of the greatest and most just of monarchs. Soldiers and citizens, of whatever nation you may be, re-establish public confidence, the source of the welfare of a state, live like brothers, render mutual aid and protection one to another, unite to defeat the intentions of the evil-minded, obey the military and civil authorities, and your tears will soon cease to flow!

With regard to supplies for the army, Napoleon decreed that all the troops in turn should enter Moscow *à la maraude* * to obtain provisions for themselves, so that the army might have its future provided for.

* As looters.

With regard to religion, Napoleon ordered the priests to be brought back and services to be again performed in the churches.

With regard to commerce and to provisioning the army, the following was placarded everywhere:

PROCLAMATION

You, peaceful inhabitants of Moscow, artisans and workmen whom misfortune has driven from the city, and you scattered tillers of the soil, still kept out in the fields by groundless fear, listen! Tranquillity is returning to this capital and order is being restored in it. Your fellow countrymen are emerging boldly from their hiding places on finding that they are respected. Any violence to them or to their property is promptly punished. His Majesty the Emperor and King protects them, and considers no one among you his enemy except those who disobey his orders. He desires to end your misfortunes and restore you to your homes and families. Respond, therefore, to his benevolent intentions and come to us without fear. Inhabitants, return with confidence to your abodes! You will soon find means of satisfying your needs. Craftsmen and industrious artisans, return to your work, your houses, your shops, where the protection of guards awaits you! You shall receive proper pay for your work. And lastly you too, peasants, come from the forests where you are hiding in terror, return to your huts without fear, in full assurance that you will find protection! Markets are established in the city where peasants can bring their surplus supplies and the products of the soil. The government has taken the following steps to ensure freedom of sale for them: (1) From today, peasants, husbandmen, and those living in the neighborhood of Moscow may without any danger bring their supplies of all kinds to two appointed markets, of which one is on the Mokhováya Street and the other at the Provision Market. (2) Such supplies will be bought from them at such prices as seller and buyer may agree on, and if a seller is unable to obtain a fair price he will be free to take his goods back to his village and no one may hinder him under any pretense. (3) Sunday and Wednesday of each week are appointed as the chief market days and to that end a sufficient number of troops will be stationed along the highroads on Tuesdays and Saturdays at such distances from the town as to protect the carts. (4) Similar measures will be taken that peasants with their carts and horses may meet with no hindrance on their return journey. (5) Steps will immediately be taken to re-establish ordinary trading.

Inhabitants of the city and villages, and you, workingmen and artisans, to whatever nation you belong, you are called on to carry out the paternal intentions of His Majesty the Emperor and King and to co-operate with him for the public welfare! Lay your respect and confidence at his feet and do not delay to unite with us!

With the object of raising the spirits of the troops and of the people, reviews were constantly held and rewards distributed. The Emperor rode through the streets to comfort the inhabitants, and, despite his preoccupation with state affairs, himself visited the theaters that were established by his order.

In regard to philanthropy, the greatest virtue of crowned heads, Napoleon also did all in his power. He caused the words *Maison de ma Mère* to be inscribed on the charitable institutions, thereby combining tender filial affection with the majestic benevolence of a monarch. He visited the Foundling Hospital and, allowing the orphans saved by him to kiss his white hands, graciously conversed with Tutólmin. Then, as Thiers eloquently recounts, he ordered his soldiers to be paid in forged Russian money which he had prepared: "Raising the use of these means by an act worthy of himself and of the French army, he let relief be distributed to those who had been burned out. But as food was too precious to be given to foreigners, who were for the most part enemies, Napoleon preferred to supply them with money with which to purchase food from outside, and had paper rubles distributed to them."

With reference to army discipline, orders were continually being issued to inflict severe punishment for the nonperformance of military duties and to suppress robbery.

CHAPTER X

But strange to say, all these measures, efforts, and plans—which were not at all worse than others issued in similar circumstances—did not affect the essence of the matter but, like the hands of a clock detached from the mechanism, swung about in an arbitrary and aimless way without engaging the cogwheels.

With reference to the military side—the plan of campaign—that work of genius of which Thiers remarks that "His genius never devised anything more profound, more skillful, or more admirable," and enters into a polemic with M. Fain to prove that this work of genius must be referred not to the fourth but to the fifteenth of October—that plan never was or could be executed, for it was quite out of touch with the facts of the case. The fortifying of the Krémlin, for which *la Mosquée* (as Napoleon termed the church of Basil the Beatified) was to have been razed to the ground, proved quite useless. The mining of the Krémlin only helped toward fulfilling Napoleon's wish that it should be blown up when he left Moscow—as a child wants the floor on which he has hurt himself to be beaten. The pursuit of the Russian army, about which Napoleon was so concerned, produced an unheard-of result. The French generals lost touch with the Russian army of sixty thousand men, and according to Thiers it was only eventually found, like a lost pin, by the skill—and apparently the genius—of Murat.

With reference to diplomacy, all Napoleon's arguments as to his magnanimity and justice, both to Tutólmin and to Yákovlev (whose chief concern was to obtain a greatcoat and a conveyance), proved useless; Alexander did not receive these envoys and did not reply to their embassage.

With regard to legal matters, after the execution of the supposed incendiaries the rest of Moscow burned down.

With regard to administrative matters, the establishment of a municipality did not stop the robberies and was only of use to certain people who formed part of that municipality and under pretext of preserving order looted Moscow or saved their own property from being looted.

With regard to religion, as to which in Egypt matters had so easily been settled by Napoleon's visit to a mosque, no results were achieved. Two or three priests who were found in Moscow did try to carry out Napoleon's wish, but one of them was slapped in the face by a French soldier while conducting service, and a French official reported of another that: "The priest whom I found and invited to say Mass cleaned and locked up the church. That night the doors were again broken open, the padlocks smashed, the books mutilated, and other disorders perpetrated."

With reference to commerce, the proclamation to industrious workmen and to peasants evoked no response. There were no industrious workmen, and the peasants caught the commissaries who ventured too far out of town with the proclamation and killed them.

As to the theaters for the entertainment of the people and the troops, these did not meet with success either. The theaters set up in the Krémlin and in Posnyákov's house were closed again at once because the actors and actresses were robbed.

Even philanthropy did not have the desired effect. The genuine as well as the false paper money which flooded Moscow lost its value. The French, collecting booty, cared only for gold. Not only was the paper money valueless which Napoleon so graciously distributed to the unfortunate, but even silver lost its value in relation to gold.

But the most amazing example of the ineffectiveness of the orders given by the authorities at that time was Napoleon's attempt to stop the looting and re-establish discipline.

This is what the army authorities were reporting:

"Looting continues in the city despite the decrees against it. Order is not yet restored and not a single merchant is carrying on trade in a lawful manner. The sutlers alone venture to trade, and they sell stolen goods."

"The neighborhood of my ward continues to be pillaged by soldiers of the 3rd Corps who, not satisfied with taking from the unfortunate inhabitants hiding in the cellars the little they have left, even have the ferocity to wound them with their sabers, as I have repeatedly witnessed."

"Nothing new, except that the soldiers are robbing and pillaging—October 9."

"Robbery and pillaging continue. There is a band of thieves in our district who ought to be arrested by a strong force—October 11."

"The Emperor is extremely displeased that despite the strict orders to stop pillage, parties of marauding Guards are continually seen returning to the Krémlin. Among the Old Guard disorder and pillage were renewed more violently than ever yesterday evening, last night, and today. The Emperor sees with regret that the picked soldiers appointed to guard his person, who should set an example of discipline, carry disobedience to such a point that they break into the cellars and stores containing army supplies. Others have disgraced themselves to the extent of disobeying sentinels and officers, and have abused and beaten them."

"The Grand Marshal of the palace," wrote the governor, "complains bitterly that in spite of repeated orders, the soldiers continue to commit nuisances in all the courtyards and even under the very windows of the Emperor."

That army, like a herd of cattle run wild and trampling underfoot the provender which might have saved it from starvation, disintegrated and perished with each additional day it remained in Moscow. But it did not go away.

It began to run away only when suddenly seized by a panic caused by the capture of transport trains on the Smolénsk road, and by the battle of Tarútino. The news of that battle of Tarútino, unexpectedly received by Napoleon at a review, evoked in him a desire to punish the Russians (Thiers says), and he issued the order for departure which the whole army was demanding.

Fleeing from Moscow the soldiers took with them everything they had stolen. Napoleon, too, carried away his own personal *trésor*, but on seeing the baggage trains that impeded the army, he was (Thiers says) horror-struck. And yet with his experience of war he did not order all the superfluous vehicles to be burned, as he had done with those of a certain marshal when approaching Moscow. He gazed at the *calèches* and carriages in which soldiers were riding and remarked that it was a very good thing, as those vehicles could be used to carry provisions, the sick, and the wounded.

The plight of the whole army resembled that of a wounded animal which feels it is perishing and does not know what it is doing. To study the skillful tactics and aims of Napoleon and his army from the time it entered Moscow till it was destroyed is like studying the dying leaps and shudders of a mortally wounded animal. Very often a wounded animal, hearing a rustle, rushes straight at the hunter's gun, runs forward and back again, and hastens its own end. Napoleon, under pressure from his whole army, did the same thing. The rustle of the battle of Tarútino frightened the beast, and it rushed forward onto the hunter's gun, reached him, turned back, and finally—like any wild beast—ran back along the most disadvantageous and dangerous path, where the old scent was familiar.

During the whole of that period Napoleon, who seems to us to have been the leader of all these movements—as the figurehead of a ship may seem to a savage to guide the vessel—acted like a child who, holding a couple of strings inside a carriage, thinks he is driving it.

CHAPTER XI

Early in the morning of the sixth of October Pierre went out of the shed, and on returning stopped by the door to play with a little blue-gray dog, with a long body and short bandy legs, that jumped about him. This little dog lived in their shed, sleeping beside Karatáev at night; it sometimes made excursions into the town but always returned again. Probably it had never had an owner, and it still belonged to nobody and had no name. The French called it Azor; the soldier who told stories called it Femgálka; Karatáev and others called it Gray, or sometimes Flabby. Its lack of a master, a name, or even of a breed or any definite color did not seem to trouble the blue-gray dog in the least. Its furry tail stood up firm and round as a plume, its bandy legs served it so well that it would often gracefully lift a hind leg and run very easily and quickly on three legs, as if disdaining to use all four. Everything pleased it. Now it would roll on its back, yelping with delight, now bask in the sun with a thoughtful air of importance, and now frolic about playing with a chip of wood or a straw.

Pierre's attire by now consisted of a dirty torn shirt (the only remnant of his former clothing), a pair of soldier's trousers which by Karatáev's advice he tied with string round the ankles for warmth, and a peasant coat and cap. Physically he had changed much during this time. He no longer seemed stout, though he still had the appearance of solidity and strength hereditary in his family. A beard and mustache covered the lower part of his face, and a tangle of hair, infested with lice, curled round his head like a cap. The look of his eyes was resolute, calm, and animatedly alert, as never before. The former slackness which had shown itself even in his eyes was now replaced by an energetic readiness for action and resistance. His feet were bare.

Pierre first looked down the field across which vehicles and horsemen were passing that morning, then into the distance across the river, then at the dog who was pretending to be in earnest about biting him, and then at his bare feet which he placed with pleasure in various positions, moving his dirty thick big toes. Every time he looked at his bare feet a smile of animated self-satisfaction flitted across his face. The sight of them reminded him of all he had experienced and learned during these weeks and this recollection was pleasant to him.

For some days the weather had been calm and clear with slight frosts in the mornings—what is called an "old wives' summer."

In the sunshine the air was warm, and that warmth was particularly pleasant with the invigorating freshness of the morning frost still in the air.

On everything—far and near—lay the magic crystal glitter seen only at that time of autumn. The Sparrow Hills were visible in the distance, with the village, the church, and the large white house. The bare trees, the sand, the bricks and roofs of the houses, the green church spire, and the corners of the white house in the distance, all stood out in the transparent air in most delicate outline and with unnatural clearness. Near by could be seen the familiar ruins of a half-burned mansion occupied by the French, with lilac bushes still showing dark green beside the fence. And even that ruined and befouled house—which in dull weather was repulsively ugly—seemed quietly beautiful now, in the clear, motionless brilliance.

A French corporal, with coat unbuttoned in a homely way, a skullcap on his head, and a short pipe in his mouth, came from behind a corner of the shed and approached Pierre with a friendly wink.

"What sunshine, Monsieur Kiril!" (Their name for Pierre.) "Eh? Just like spring!"

And the corporal leaned against the door and offered Pierre his pipe, though whenever he offered it Pierre always declined it.

"To be on the march in such weather..." he began.

Pierre inquired what was being said about leaving, and the corporal told him that nearly all the troops were starting and there ought to be an order about the prisoners that day. Sokolóv, one of the soldiers in the shed with Pierre, was dying, and Pierre told the corporal that something should be done about him. The corporal replied that Pierre need not worry about that as they had an ambulance and a permanent hospital and arrangements would be made for the sick, and that in general everything that could happen had been foreseen by the authorities.

"Besides, Monsieur Kiril, you have only to say a word to the captain, you know. He is a man who never forgets anything. Speak to the captain when he makes his round, he will do anything for you."

(The captain of whom the corporal spoke often had long chats with Pierre and showed him all sorts of favors.)

"'You see, St. Thomas,' he said to me the other day. 'Monsieur Kiril is a man of education, who speaks French. He is a Russian seigneur who has had misfortunes, but he is a man. He knows what's what.... If he wants anything and asks me, he won't get a refusal. When one has studied, you see, one likes education and well-bred people.' It is for your sake I mention it, Monsieur Kiril. The other day if it had not been for you that affair would have ended ill."

And after chatting a while longer, the corporal went away. (The affair he had alluded to had happened a few days before—a fight between the prisoners and the French soldiers, in which Pierre had succeeded in pacifying his comrades.) Some of the prisoners who had heard Pierre talking to the corporal immediately asked what the Frenchman had said. While Pierre was repeating what he had been told about the army leaving Moscow, a thin, sallow, tattered French soldier came up to the door of the shed. Rapidly and timidly raising his fingers to his forehead by way of greeting, he asked Pierre whether the soldier Platoche to whom he had given a shirt to sew was in that shed.

A week before the French had had boot leather and linen issued to them, which they had given out to the prisoners to make up into boots and shirts for them.

"Ready, ready, dear fellow!" said Karatáev, coming out with a neatly folded shirt.

Karatáev, on account of the warm weather and for convenience at work, was wearing only trousers and a tattered shirt as black as soot. His hair was bound round, workman fashion, with a wisp of lime-tree bast, and his round face seemed rounder and pleasanter than ever.

"A promise is own brother to performance! I said Friday and here it is, ready," said Platón, smiling and unfolding the shirt he had sewn.

The Frenchman glanced around uneasily and then, as if overcoming his hesitation, rapidly threw off his uniform and put on the shirt. He had a long, greasy, flowered silk waistcoat next to his sallow, thin bare body, but no shirt. He was evidently afraid the prisoners looking on would laugh at him, and thrust his head into the shirt hurriedly. None of the prisoners said a word.

"See, it fits well!" Platón kept repeating, pulling the shirt straight.

The Frenchman, having pushed his head and hands through, without raising his eyes, looked down at the shirt and examined the seams.

"You see, dear man, this is not a sewing shop, and I had no proper tools; and, as they say, one needs a tool even to kill a louse," said Platón with one of his round smiles, obviously pleased with his work.

"It's good, quite good, thank you," said the Frenchman, in French, "but there must be some linen left over."

"It will fit better still when it sets to your body," said Karatáev, still admiring his handiwork. "You'll be nice and comfortable...."

"Thanks, thanks, old fellow.... But the bits left over?" said the Frenchman again and smiled. He took out an assignation ruble note and gave it to Karatáev. "But give me the pieces that are over."

Pierre saw that Platón did not want to understand what the Frenchman was saying, and he looked on without interfering. Karatáev thanked the Frenchman for the money and went on admiring his own work. The Frenchman insisted on having the pieces returned that were left over and asked Pierre to translate what he said.

"What does he want the bits for?" said Karatáev. "They'd make fine leg bands for us. Well, never mind."

And Karatáev, with a suddenly changed and saddened expression, took a small bundle of scraps from inside his shirt and gave it to the Frenchman without looking at him. "Oh dear!" muttered Karatáev and went away. The Frenchman looked at the linen, considered for a moment, then looked inquiringly at Pierre and, as if Pierre's look had told him something, suddenly blushed and shouted in a squeaky voice:

"Platoche! Eh, Platoche! Keep them yourself!" And handing back the odd bits he turned and went out.

"There, look at that," said Karatáev, swaying his head. "People said they were not Christians, but they too have souls. It's what the old folk used to say: 'A sweating hand's an open hand, a dry hand's close.' He's naked, but yet he's given it back."

Karatáev smiled thoughtfully and was silent awhile looking at the pieces.

"But they'll make grand leg bands, dear friend," he said, and went back into the shed.

CHAPTER XII

Four weeks had passed since Pierre had been taken prisoner and though the French had offered to move him from the men's to the officers' shed, he had stayed in the shed where he was first put.

In burned and devastated Moscow Pierre experienced almost the extreme limits of privation a man can endure; but thanks to his physical strength and health, of which he had till then been unconscious, and thanks especially to the fact that the privations came so gradually that it was impossible to say when they began, he endured his position not only lightly but joyfully. And just at this time he obtained the tranquillity and ease of mind he had formerly striven in vain to reach. He had long sought in different ways that tranquillity of mind, that inner harmony which had so impressed him in the soldiers at the battle of Borodinó. He had sought it in philanthropy, in Freemasonry, in the dissipations of town life, in wine, in heroic feats of self-sacrifice, and in romantic love for Natásha; he had sought it by reasoning—and all these quests and experiments had failed him. And now without thinking about it he had found that peace and inner harmony only through the horror of death, through privation, and through what he recognized in Karatáev.

Those dreadful moments he had lived through at the executions had as it were forever washed away from his imagination and memory the agitating thoughts and feelings that had formerly seemed so important. It did not now occur to him to think of Russia, or the war, or politics, or Napoleon. It was plain to him that all these things were no business of his, and that he was not called on to judge concerning them and therefore could not do so. "Russia and summer weather are not bound together," he thought, repeating words of Karatáev's which he found strangely consoling. His intention of killing Napoleon and his calculations of the cabalistic number of the beast of the Apocalypse now seemed to him meaningless and even ridiculous. His anger with his wife and anxiety that his name should not be smirched now seemed not merely trivial but even amusing. What concern was it of his that somewhere or other that woman was leading the life she preferred? What did it matter to anybody, and especially to him, whether or not they found out that their prisoner's name was Count Bezúkhov?

He now often remembered his conversation with Prince Andrew and quite agreed with him, though he understood Prince Andrew's thoughts somewhat differently. Prince Andrew had thought and said that happiness could only be negative, but had said it with a shade of bitterness and irony as though he was really saying that all desire for positive happiness is implanted in us merely to torment us and never be satisfied. But Pierre believed it without any mental reservation. The absence of suffering, the satisfaction of one's needs and consequent freedom in the choice of one's occupation, that is, of one's way of life, now seemed to Pierre to be indubitably man's highest happiness. Here and now for the first time he fully appreciated the enjoyment of eating when he wanted to eat, drinking when he wanted to drink, sleeping when he wanted to sleep, of warmth when he was cold, of talking to a fellow man when he wished to talk and to hear a human voice. The satisfaction of one's needs—good food, cleanliness, and freedom—now that he was deprived of all this, seemed to Pierre to constitute perfect happiness; and the choice of occupation, that is, of his way of life—now that that was so restricted—seemed to him such an easy matter that he forgot that a superfluity of the comforts of life destroys all joy in satisfying one's needs, while great freedom in the choice of occupation—such freedom as his wealth, his education, and his social position had given him in his own life—is just what makes the choice of occupation insolubly difficult and destroys the desire and possibility of having an occupation.

All Pierre's daydreams now turned on the time when he would be free. Yet subsequently, and for the rest of his life, he thought and spoke with enthusiasm of that month of captivity, of those irrecoverable, strong, joyful sensations, and chiefly of the complete peace of mind and inner freedom which he experienced only during those weeks.

When on the first day he got up early, went out of the shed at dawn, and saw the cupolas and crosses of the New Convent of the Virgin still dark at first, the hoarfrost on the dusty grass, the Sparrow Hills, and the wooded banks above the winding river vanishing in the purple distance, when he felt the contact of the fresh air and heard the noise of the crows flying from Moscow across the field, and when afterwards light gleamed from the east and the sun's rim appeared solemnly from behind a cloud, and the cupolas and crosses, the hoarfrost, the distance and the river, all began to sparkle in the glad light—Pierre felt a new joy and strength in life such as he had never before known. And this not only stayed with him during the whole of his imprisonment, but even grew in strength as the hardships of his position increased.

That feeling of alertness and of readiness for anything was still further strengthened in him by the high opinion his fellow prisoners formed of him soon after his arrival at the shed. With his knowledge of languages, the respect shown him by the French, his simplicity, his readiness to give anything asked of him (he received the allowance of three rubles a week made to officers); with his strength, which he showed to the soldiers by pressing nails into the walls of the hut; his gentleness to his companions, and his capacity for sitting still and thinking without doing anything (which seemed to them incomprehensible), he appeared to them a rather mysterious and superior being. The very qualities that had been a hindrance, if not actually harmful, to him in the world he had lived in—his strength, his disdain for the comforts of life, his absent-mindedness and simplicity—here among these people gave him almost the status of a hero. And Pierre felt that their opinion placed responsibilities upon him.

CHAPTER XIII

The French evacuation began on the night between the sixth and seventh of October: kitchens and sheds were dismantled, carts loaded, and troops and baggage trains started.

At seven in the morning a French convoy in marching trim, wearing shakos and carrying muskets, knapsacks, and enormous sacks, stood in front of the sheds, and animated French talk mingled with curses sounded all along the lines.

In the shed everyone was ready, dressed, belted, shod, and only awaited the order to start. The sick soldier, Sokolóv, pale and thin with dark shadows round his eyes, alone sat in his place barefoot and not dressed. His eyes, prominent from the emaciation of his face, gazed inquiringly at his comrades who were paying no attention to him, and he moaned regularly and quietly. It was evidently not so much his sufferings that caused him to moan (he had dysentery) as his fear and grief at being left alone.

Pierre, girt with a rope round his waist and wearing shoes Karatáev had made for him from some leather a French soldier had torn off a tea chest and brought to have his boots mended with, went up to the sick man and squatted down beside him.

"You know, Sokolóv, they are not all going away! They have a hospital here. You may be better off than we others," said Pierre.

"O Lord! Oh, it will be the death of me! O Lord!" moaned the man in a louder voice.

"I'll go and ask them again directly," said Pierre, rising and going to the door of the shed.

Just as Pierre reached the door, the corporal who had offered him a pipe the day before came up to it with two soldiers. The corporal and soldiers were in marching kit with knapsacks and shakos that had metal straps, and these changed their familiar faces.

The corporal came, according to orders, to shut the door. The prisoners had to be counted before being let out.

"Corporal, what will they do with the sick man?..." Pierre began.

But even as he spoke he began to doubt whether this was the corporal he knew or a stranger, so unlike himself did the corporal seem at that moment. Moreover, just as Pierre was speaking a sharp rattle of drums was suddenly heard from both sides. The corporal frowned at Pierre's words and, uttering some meaningless oaths, slammed the door. The shed became semidark, and the sharp rattle of the drums on two sides drowned the sick man's groans.

"There it is!... *It* again!..." said Pierre to himself, and an involuntary shudder ran down his spine. In the corporal's changed face, in the sound of his voice, in the stirring and deafening noise of the drums, he recognized that mysterious, callous force which compelled people against their will to kill their fellow men—that force the effect of which he had witnessed during the executions. To fear or to try to escape that force, to address entreaties or exhortations to those who served as its tools, was useless. Pierre knew this now. One had to wait and endure. He did not again go to the sick man, nor turn to look at him, but stood frowning by the door of the hut.

When that door was opened and the prisoners, crowding against one another like a flock of sheep, squeezed into the exit, Pierre pushed his way forward and approached that very captain who as the corporal had assured him was ready to do anything for him. The captain was also in marching kit, and on his cold face appeared that same *it* which Pierre had recognized in the corporal's words and in the roll of the drums.

"Pass on, pass on!" the captain reiterated, frowning sternly, and looking at the prisoners who thronged past him.

Pierre went up to him, though he knew his attempt would be vain.

"What now?" the officer asked with a cold look as if not recognizing Pierre.

Pierre told him about the sick man.

"He'll manage to walk, devil take him!" said the captain. "Pass on, pass on!" he continued without looking at Pierre.

"But he is dying," Pierre again began.

"Be so good..." shouted the captain, frowning angrily.

"Dram-da-da-dam, dam-dam..." rattled the drums, and Pierre understood that this mysterious force completely controlled these men and that it was now useless to say any more.

The officer prisoners were separated from the soldiers and told to march in front. There were about thirty officers, with Pierre among them, and about three hundred men.

The officers, who had come from the other sheds, were all strangers to Pierre and much better dressed than he. They looked at him and at his shoes mistrustfully, as at an alien. Not far from him walked a fat major with a sallow, bloated, angry face, who was wearing a Kazán dressing gown tied round with a towel, and who evidently enjoyed the respect of his fellow prisoners. He kept one hand, in which he clasped his tobacco pouch, inside the bosom of his dressing gown and held the stem of his pipe firmly with the other. Panting and puffing, the major grumbled and growled at everybody because he thought he was being pushed and that they were all hurrying when they had nowhere to hurry to and were all surprised at something when there was nothing to be surprised at. Another, a thin little officer, was speaking to everyone, conjecturing where they were now being taken and how far they would get that day. An official in felt boots and wearing a commissariat uniform ran round from side to side and gazed at the ruins of Moscow, loudly announcing his observations as to what had been burned down and what this or that part of the city was that they could see. A third officer, who by his accent was a Pole, disputed with the commissariat officer, arguing that he was mistaken in his identification of the different wards of Moscow.

"What are you disputing about?" said the major angrily. "What does it matter whether it is St. Nicholas or St. Blasius? You see it's burned down, and there's an end of it.... What are you pushing for? Isn't the road wide enough?" said he, turning to a man behind him who was not pushing him at all.

"Oh, oh, oh! What have they done?" the prisoners on one side and another were heard saying as they gazed on the charred ruins. "All beyond the river, and Zúbova, and in the Krémlin.... Just look! There's not half of it left. Yes, I told you—the whole quarter beyond the river, and so it is."

"Well, you know it's burned, so what's the use of talking?" said the major.

As they passed near a church in the Khamóvniki (one of the few unburned quarters of Moscow) the whole mass of prisoners suddenly started to one side and exclamations of horror and disgust were heard.

"Ah, the villains! What heathens! Yes; dead, dead, so he is... And smeared with something!"

Pierre too drew near the church where the thing was that evoked these exclamations, and dimly made out something leaning against the palings surrounding the church. From the words of his comrades who saw better than he did, he found that this was the body of a man, set upright against the palings with its face smeared with soot.

"Go on! What the devil... Go on! Thirty thousand devils!..." the convoy guards began cursing and the French soldiers, with fresh virulence, drove away with their swords the crowd of prisoners who were gazing at the dead man.

CHAPTER XIV

Through the cross streets of the Khamóvniki quarter the prisoners marched, followed only by their escort and the vehicles and wagons belonging to that escort, but when they reached the supply stores they came among a huge and closely packed train of artillery mingled with private vehicles.

At the bridge they all halted, waiting for those in front to get across. From the bridge they had a view of endless lines of moving baggage trains before and behind them. To the right, where the Kalúga road turns near Neskúchny, endless rows of troops and carts stretched away into the distance. These were troops of Beauharnais' corps which had started before any of the others. Behind, along the riverside and across the Stone Bridge, were Ney's troops and transport.

Davout's troops, in whose charge were the prisoners, were crossing the Crimean bridge and some were already debouching into the Kalúga road. But the baggage trains stretched out so that the last of Beauharnais' train had not yet got out of Moscow and reached the Kalúga road when the vanguard of Ney's army was already emerging from the Great Ordýnka Street.

When they had crossed the Crimean bridge the prisoners moved a few steps forward, halted, and again moved on, and from all sides vehicles and men crowded closer and closer together. They advanced the few hundred paces that separated the bridge from the Kalúga road, taking more than an hour to do so, and came out upon the square where the streets of the Transmoskvá ward and the Kalúga road converge, and the prisoners jammed close together had to stand for some hours at that crossway. From all sides, like the roar of the sea, were heard the rattle of wheels, the tramp of feet, and incessant shouts of anger and abuse. Pierre stood pressed against the wall of a charred house, listening to that noise which mingled in his imagination with the roll of the drums.

To get a better view, several officer prisoners climbed onto the wall of the half-burned house against which Pierre was leaning.

"What crowds! Just look at the crowds!... They've loaded goods even on the cannon! Look there, those are furs!" they exclaimed. "Just see what the blackguards have looted.... There! See what that one has behind in the cart.... Why, those are settings taken from some icons, by heaven!... Oh, the rascals!... See how that fellow has loaded himself up, he can hardly walk! Good lord, they've even grabbed those chaises!... See that fellow there sitting on the trunks.... Heavens! They're fighting."

"That's right, hit him on the snout—on his snout! Like this, we shan't get away before evening. Look, look there.... Why, that must be Napoleon's own. See what horses! And the monograms with a crown! It's like a portable house.... That fellow's dropped his sack and doesn't see it. Fighting again... A woman with a baby, and not bad-looking either! Yes, I dare say, that's the way they'll let you pass.... Just look, there's no end to it. Russian wenches, by heaven, so they are! In carriages—see how comfortably they've settled themselves!"

Again, as at the church in Khamóvniki, a wave of general curiosity bore all the prisoners forward onto the road, and Pierre, thanks to his stature, saw over the heads of the others what so attracted their curiosity. In three carriages involved among the munition carts, closely squeezed together, sat women with rouged faces, dressed in glaring colors, who were shouting something in shrill voices.

From the moment Pierre had recognized the appearance of the mysterious force nothing had seemed to him strange or dreadful: neither the corpse smeared with soot for fun nor these women hurrying away nor the burned ruins of Moscow. All that he now witnessed scarcely made an impression on him—as if his soul, making ready for a hard struggle, refused to receive impressions that might weaken it.

The women's vehicles drove by. Behind them came more carts, soldiers, wagons, soldiers, gun carriages, carriages, soldiers, ammunition carts, more soldiers, and now and then women.

Pierre did not see the people as individuals but saw their movement.

All these people and horses seemed driven forward by some invisible power. During the hour Pierre watched them they all came flowing from the different streets with one and the same desire to get on quickly; they all jostled one another, began to grow angry and to fight, white teeth gleamed, brows frowned, ever the same words of abuse flew from side to side, and all the faces bore the same swaggeringly resolute and coldly cruel expression that had struck Pierre that morning on the corporal's face when the drums were beating.

It was not till nearly evening that the officer commanding the escort collected his men and with shouts and quarrels forced his way in among the baggage trains, and the prisoners, hemmed in on all sides, emerged onto the Kalúga road.

They marched very quickly, without resting, and halted only when the sun began to set. The baggage carts drew up close together and the men began to prepare for their night's rest. They all appeared angry and dissatisfied. For a long time, oaths, angry shouts, and fighting could be heard from all sides. A carriage that followed the escort ran into one of the carts and knocked a hole in it with its pole. Several soldiers ran toward the cart from different sides: some beat the carriage horses on their heads, turning them aside, others fought among themselves, and Pierre saw that one German was badly wounded on the head by a sword.

It seemed that all these men, now that they had stopped amid fields in the chill dusk of the autumn evening, experienced one and the same feeling of unpleasant awakening from the hurry and eagerness to push on that had seized them at the start. Once at a standstill they all seemed to understand that they did not yet know where they were going, and that much that was painful and difficult awaited them on this journey.

During this halt the escort treated the prisoners even worse than they had done at the start. It was here that the prisoners for the first time received horseflesh for their meat ration.

From the officer down to the lowest soldier they showed what seemed like personal spite against each of the prisoners, in unexpected contrast to their former friendly relations.

This spite increased still more when, on calling over the roll of prisoners, it was found that in the bustle of leaving Moscow one Russian soldier, who had pretended to suffer from colic, had escaped. Pierre saw a Frenchman beat a Russian soldier cruelly for straying too far from the road, and heard his friend the captain reprimand and threaten to court-martial a noncommissioned officer on account of the escape of the Russian. To the noncommissioned officer's excuse that the prisoner was ill and could not walk, the officer replied that the order was to shoot those who lagged behind. Pierre felt that that fatal force which had crushed him during the executions, but which he had not felt during his imprisonment, now again controlled his existence. It was terrible, but he felt that in proportion to the efforts of that fatal force to crush him, there grew and strengthened in his soul a power of life independent of it.

He ate his supper of buckwheat soup with horseflesh and chatted with his comrades.

Neither Pierre nor any of the others spoke of what they had seen in Moscow, or of the roughness of their treatment by the French, or of the order to shoot them which had been announced to them. As if in reaction against the worsening of their position they were all particularly animated and gay. They spoke of personal reminiscences, of amusing scenes they had witnessed during the campaign, and avoided all talk of their present situation.

The sun had set long since. Bright stars shone out here and there in the sky. A red glow as of a conflagration spread above the horizon from the rising full moon, and that vast red ball swayed strangely in the gray haze. It grew light. The evening was ending, but the night had not yet come. Pierre got up and left his new companions, crossing between the campfires to the other side of the road where he had been told the common soldier prisoners were stationed. He wanted to talk to them. On the road he was stopped by a French sentinel who ordered him back.

Pierre turned back, not to his companions by the campfire, but to an unharnessed cart where there was nobody. Tucking his legs under him and dropping his head he sat down on the cold ground by the wheel of the cart and remained motionless a long while sunk in thought. Suddenly he burst out into a fit of his broad, good-natured laughter, so loud that men from various sides turned with surprise to see what this strange and evidently solitary laughter could mean.

"Ha-ha-ha!" laughed Pierre. And he said aloud to himself: "The soldier did not let me pass. They took me and shut me up. They hold me captive. What, me? Me? My immortal soul? Ha-ha-ha! Ha-ha-ha!..." and he laughed till tears started to his eyes.

A man got up and came to see what this queer big fellow was laughing at all by himself. Pierre stopped laughing, got up, went farther away from the inquisitive man, and looked around him.

The huge, endless bivouac that had previously resounded with the crackling of campfires and the voices of many men had grown quiet, the red campfires were growing paler and dying down. High up in the light sky hung the full moon. Forests and fields beyond the camp, unseen before, were now visible in the distance. And farther still, beyond those forests and fields, the bright, oscillating, limitless distance lured one to itself. Pierre glanced up at the sky and the twinkling stars in its faraway depths. "And all that is me, all that is within me, and it is all I!" thought Pierre. "And they caught all that and put it into a shed boarded up with planks!" He smiled, and went and lay down to sleep beside his companions.

CHAPTER XV

In the early days of October another envoy came to Kutúzov with a letter from Napoleon proposing peace and falsely dated from Moscow, though Napoleon was already not far from Kutúzov on the old Kalúga road. Kutúzov replied to this letter as he had done to the one formerly brought by Lauriston, saying that there could be no question of peace.

Soon after that a report was received from Dórokhov's guerrilla detachment operating to the left of Tarútino that troops of Broussier's division had been seen at Formínsk and that being separated from the rest of the French army they might easily be destroyed. The soldiers and officers again demanded action. Generals on the staff, excited by the memory of the easy victory at Tarútino, urged Kutúzov to carry out Dórokhov's suggestion. Kutúzov did not consider any offensive necessary. The result was a compromise which was inevitable: a small detachment was sent to Formínsk to attack Broussier.

By a strange coincidence, this task, which turned out to be a most difficult and important one, was entrusted to Dokhtúrov—that same modest little Dokhtúrov whom no one had described to us as drawing up plans of battles, dashing about in front of regiments, showering crosses on batteries, and so on, and who was thought to be and was spoken of as undecided and undiscerning—but whom we find commanding wherever the position was most difficult all through the Russo-French wars from Austerlitz to the year 1813. At Austerlitz he remained last at the Augezd dam, rallying the regiments, saving what was possible when all were flying and perishing and not a single general was left in the rear guard. Ill with fever he went to

Smolénsk with twenty thousand men to defend the town against Napoleon's whole army. In Smolénsk, at the Malákhov Gate, he had hardly dozed off in a paroxysm of fever before he was awakened by the bombardment of the town—and Smolénsk held out all day long. At the battle of Borodinó, when Bagratión was killed and nine tenths of the men of our left flank had fallen and the full force of the French artillery fire was directed against it, the man sent there was this same irresolute and undiscerning Dokhtúrov—Kutúzov hastening to rectify a mistake he had made by sending someone else there first. And the quiet little Dokhtúrov rode thither, and Borodinó became the greatest glory of the Russian army. Many heroes have been described to us in verse and prose, but of Dokhtúrov scarcely a word has been said.

It was Dokhtúrov again whom they sent to Formínsk and from there to Málo-Yaroslávets, the place where the last battle with the French was fought and where the obvious disintegration of the French army began; and we are told of many geniuses and heroes of that period of the campaign, but of Dokhtúrov nothing or very little is said and that dubiously. And this silence about Dokhtúrov is the clearest testimony to his merit.

It is natural for a man who does not understand the workings of a machine to imagine that a shaving that has fallen into it by chance and is interfering with its action and tossing about in it is its most important part. The man who does not understand the construction of the machine cannot conceive that the small connecting cogwheel which revolves quietly is one of the most essential parts of the machine, and not the shaving which merely harms and hinders the working.

On the tenth of October when Dokhtúrov had gone halfway to Formínsk and stopped at the village of Aristóvo, preparing faithfully to execute the orders he had received, the whole French army having, in its convulsive movement, reached Murat's position apparently in order to give battle—suddenly without any reason turned off to the left onto the new Kalúga road and began to enter Formínsk, where only Broussier had been till then. At that time Dokhtúrov had under his command, besides Dórokhov's detachment, the two small guerrilla detachments of Figner and Seslávin.

On the evening of October 11 Seslávin came to the Aristóvo headquarters with a French guardsman he had captured. The prisoner said that the troops that had entered Formínsk that day were the vanguard of the whole army, that Napoleon was there and the whole army had left Moscow four days previously. That same evening a house serf who had come from Bórovsk said he had seen an immense army entering the town. Some Cossacks of Dokhtúrov's detachment reported having sighted the French Guards marching along the road to Bórovsk. From all these reports it was evident that where they had expected to meet a single division there was now the whole French army marching from Moscow in an unexpected direction—along the Kalúga road. Dokhtúrov was unwilling to undertake any action, as it was not clear to him now what he ought to do. He had been ordered to attack Formínsk. But only Broussier had been there at that time and now the whole French army was there. Ermólov wished to act on his own judgment, but Dokhtúrov insisted that he must have Kutúzov's instructions. So it was decided to send a dispatch to the staff.

For this purpose a capable officer, Bolkhovítinov, was chosen, who was to explain the whole affair by word of mouth, besides delivering a written report. Toward midnight Bolkhovítinov, having received the dispatch and verbal instructions, galloped off to the General Staff accompanied by a Cossack with spare horses.

CHAPTER XVI

It was a warm, dark, autumn night. It had been raining for four days. Having changed horses twice and galloped twenty miles in an hour and a half over a sticky, muddy road, Bolkhovítinov reached Litashëvka after one o'clock at night. Dismounting at a cottage on whose wattle fence hung a signboard, GENERAL STAFF, and throwing down his reins, he entered a dark passage.

"The general on duty, quick! It's very important!" said he to someone who had risen and was sniffing in the dark passage.

"He has been very unwell since the evening and this is the third night he has not slept," said the orderly pleadingly in a whisper. "You should wake the captain first."

"But this is very important, from General Dokhtúrov," said Bolkhovítinov, entering the open door which he had found by feeling in the dark.

The orderly had gone in before him and began waking somebody.

"Your honor, your honor! A courier."

"What? What's that? From whom?" came a sleepy voice.

"From Dokhtúrov and from AlexéyPetróvich. Napoleon is at Formínsk," said Bolkhovítinov, unable to see in the dark who was speaking but guessing by the voice that it was not Konovnítsyn.

The man who had wakened yawned and stretched himself.

"I don't like waking him," he said, fumbling for something. "He is very ill. Perhaps this is only a rumor."

"Here is the dispatch," said Bolkhovítinov. "My orders are to give it at once to the general on duty."

"Wait a moment, I'll light a candle. You damned rascal, where do you always hide it?" said the voice of the man who was stretching himself, to the orderly. (This was Shcherbínin, Konovnítsyn's adjutant.) "I've found it, I've found it!" he added.

The orderly was striking a light and Shcherbínin was fumbling for something on the candlestick.

"Oh, the nasty beasts!" said he with disgust.

By the light of the sparks Bolkhovítinov saw Shcherbínin's youthful face as he held the candle, and the face of another man who was still asleep. This was Konovnítsyn.

When the flame of the sulphur splinters kindled by the tinder burned up, first blue and then red, Shcherbínin lit the tallow candle, from the candlestick of which the cockroaches that had been gnawing it were running away, and looked at the messenger. Bolkhovítinov was bespattered all over with mud and had smeared his face by wiping it with his sleeve.

"Who gave the report?" inquired Shcherbínin, taking the envelope.

"The news is reliable," said Bolkhovítinov. "Prisoners, Cossacks, and the scouts all say the same thing."

"There's nothing to be done, we'll have to wake him," said Shcherbínin, rising and going up to the man in the nightcap who lay covered by a greatcoat. "Peter Petróvich!" said he. (Konovnítsyn did not stir.) "To the General Staff!" he said with a smile, knowing that those words would be sure to arouse him.

And in fact the head in the nightcap was lifted at once. On Konovnítsyn's handsome, resolute face with cheeks flushed by fever, there still remained for an instant a faraway dreamy expression remote from present affairs, but then he suddenly started and his face assumed its habitual calm and firm appearance.

"Well, what is it? From whom?" he asked immediately but without hurry, blinking at the light.

While listening to the officer's report Konovnítsyn broke the seal and read the dispatch. Hardly had he done so before he lowered his legs in their woolen stockings to the earthen floor and began putting on his boots. Then he took off his nightcap, combed his hair over his temples, and donned his cap.

"Did you get here quickly? Let us go to his Highness."

Konovnítsyn had understood at once that the news brought was of great importance and that no time must be lost. He did not consider or ask himself whether the news was good or bad. That did not interest him. He regarded the whole business of the war not with his intelligence or his reason but by something else. There was within him a deep unexpressed conviction that all would be well, but that one must not trust to this and still less speak about it, but must only attend to one's own work. And he did his work, giving his whole strength to the task.

Peter PetróvichKonovnítsyn, like Dokhtúrov, seems to have been included merely for propriety's sake in the list of the so-called heroes of 1812—the Barclays, Raévskis, Ermólovs, Plátovs, and Milorádoviches. Like Dokhtúrov he had the reputation of being a man of very limited capacity and information, and like Dokhtúrov he never made plans of battle but was always found where the situation was most difficult. Since his appointment as general on duty he had always slept with his door open, giving orders that every messenger should be allowed to wake him up. In battle he was always under fire, so that Kutúzov reproved him for it and feared to send him to the front, and like Dokhtúrov he was one of those unnoticed cogwheels that, without clatter or noise, constitute the most essential part of the machine.

Coming out of the hut into the damp, dark night Konovnítsyn frowned—partly from an increased pain in his head and partly at the unpleasant thought that occurred to him, of how all that nest of influential men on the staff would be stirred up by this news, especially Bennigsen, who ever since Tarútino had been at daggers drawn with Kutúzov; and how they would make suggestions, quarrel, issue orders, and rescind them. And this premonition was disagreeable to him though he knew it could not be helped.

And in fact Toll, to whom he went to communicate the news, immediately began to expound his plans to a general sharing his quarters, until Konovnítsyn, who listened in weary silence, reminded him that they must go to see his Highness.

CHAPTER XVII

Kutúzov like all old people did not sleep much at night. He often fell asleep unexpectedly in the daytime, but at night, lying on his bed without undressing, he generally remained awake thinking.

So he lay now on his bed, supporting his large, heavy, scarred head on his plump hand, with his one eye open, meditating and peering into the darkness.

Since Bennigsen, who corresponded with the Emperor and had more influence than anyone else on the staff, had begun to avoid him, Kutúzov was more at ease as to the possibility of himself and his troops being obliged to take part in useless aggressive movements. The lesson of the Tarútino battle and of the day before it, which Kutúzov remembered with pain, must, he thought, have some effect on others too.

"They must understand that we can only lose by taking the offensive. Patience and time are my warriors, my champions," thought Kutúzov. He knew that an apple should not be plucked while it is green. It will fall of itself when ripe, but if picked unripe the apple is spoiled, the tree is harmed, and your teeth are set on edge. Like an experienced sportsman he knew that the beast was wounded, and wounded as only the whole strength of Russia could have wounded it, but whether it was mortally wounded or not was still an undecided question. Now by the fact of Lauriston and Barthélemi having been sent, and by the reports of the guerrillas, Kutúzov was almost sure that the wound was mortal. But he needed further proofs and it was necessary to wait.

"They want to run to see how they have wounded it. Wait and we shall see! Continual maneuvers, continual advances!" thought he. "What for? Only to distinguish themselves! As if fighting were fun.

They are like children from whom one can't get any sensible account of what has happened because they all want to show how well they can fight. But that's not what is needed now.

"And what ingenious maneuvers they all propose to me! It seems to them that when they have thought of two or three contingencies" (he remembered the general plan sent him from Petersburg) "they have foreseen everything. But the contingencies are endless."

The undecided question as to whether the wound inflicted at Borodinó was mortal or not had hung over Kutúzov's head for a whole month. On the one hand the French had occupied Moscow. On the other Kutúzov felt assured with all his being that the terrible blow into which he and all the Russians had put their whole strength must have been mortal. But in any case proofs were needed; he had waited a whole month for them and grew more impatient the longer he waited. Lying on his bed during those sleepless nights he did just what he reproached those younger generals for doing. He imagined all sorts of possible contingencies, just like the younger men, but with this difference, that he saw thousands of contingencies instead of two or three and based nothing on them. The longer he thought the more contingencies presented themselves. He imagined all sorts of movements of the Napoleonic army as a whole or in sections—against Petersburg, or against him, or to outflank him. He thought too of the possibility (which he feared most of all) that Napoleon might fight him with his own weapon and remain in Moscow awaiting him. Kutúzov even imagined that Napoleon's army might turn back through Medýn and Yukhnóv, but the one thing he could not foresee was what happened—the insane, convulsive stampede of Napoleon's army during its first eleven days after leaving Moscow: a stampede which made possible what Kutúzov had not yet even dared to think of—the complete extermination of the French. Dórokhov's report about Broussier'sdivision, the guerrillas' reports of distress in Napoleon's army, rumors of preparations for leaving Moscow, all confirmed the supposition that the French army was beaten and preparing for flight. But these were only suppositions, which seemed important to the younger men but not to Kutúzov. With his sixty years' experience he knew what value to attach to rumors, knew how apt people who desire anything are to group all news so that it appears to confirm what they desire, and he knew how readily in such cases they omit all that makes for the contrary. And the more he desired it the less he allowed himself to believe it. This question absorbed all his mental powers. All else was to him only life's customary routine. To such customary routine belonged his conversations with the staff, the letters he wrote from Tarútino to Madame de Staël, the reading of novels, the distribution of awards, his correspondence with Petersburg, and so on. But the destruction of the French, which he alone foresaw, was his heart's one desire.

On the night of the eleventh of October he lay leaning on his arm and thinking of that.

There was a stir in the next room and he heard the steps of Toll, Konovnítsyn, and Bolkhovítinov.

"Eh, who's there? Come in, come in! What news?" the field marshal called out to them.

While a footman was lighting a candle, Toll communicated the substance of the news.

"Who brought it?" asked Kutúzov with a look which, when the candle was lit, struck Toll by its cold severity.

"There can be no doubt about it, your Highness."

"Call him in, call him here."

Kutúzov sat up with one leg hanging down from the bed and his big paunch resting against the other which was doubled under him. He screwed up his seeing eye to scrutinize the messenger more carefully, as if wishing to read in his face what preoccupied his own mind.

"Tell me, tell me, friend," said he to Bolkhovítinov in his low, aged voice, as he pulled together the shirt which gaped open on his chest, "come nearer—nearer. What news have you brought me? Eh? That Napoleon has left Moscow? Are you sure? Eh?"

Bolkhovítinov gave a detailed account from the beginning of all he had been told to report.

"Speak quicker, quicker! Don't torture me!" Kutúzov interrupted him.

Bolkhovítinov told him everything and was then silent, awaiting instructions. Toll was beginning to say something but Kutúzov checked him. He tried to say something, but his face suddenly puckered and wrinkled; he waved his arm at Toll and turned to the opposite side of the room, to the corner darkened by the icons that hung there.

"O Lord, my Creator, Thou has heard our prayer..." said he in a tremulous voice with folded hands. "Russia is saved. I thank Thee, O Lord!" and he wept.

CHAPTER XVIII

From the time he received this news to the end of the campaign all Kutúzov's activity was directed toward restraining his troops, by authority, by guile, and by entreaty, from useless attacks, maneuvers, or encounters with the perishing enemy. Dokhtúrov went to Málo-Yaroslávets, but Kutúzov lingered with the main army and gave orders for the evacuation of Kalúga—a retreat beyond which town seemed to him quite possible.

Everywhere Kutúzov retreated, but the enemy without waiting for his retreat fled in the opposite direction.

Napoleon's historians describe to us his skilled maneuvers at Tarútino and Málo-Yaroslávets, and make conjectures as to what would have happened had Napoleon been in time to penetrate into the rich southern provinces.

But not to speak of the fact that nothing prevented him from advancing into those southern provinces (for the Russian army did not bar his way), the historians forget that nothing could have saved his army, for then already it bore within itself the germs of inevitable ruin. How could that army—which had found abundant supplies in Moscow and had trampled them underfoot instead of keeping them, and on arriving at Smolénsk had looted provisions instead of storing them—how could that army recuperate in Kalúga province, which was inhabited by Russians such as those who lived in Moscow, and where fire had the same property of consuming what was set ablaze?

That army could not recover anywhere. Since the battle of Borodinó and the pillage of Moscow it had borne within itself, as it were, the chemical elements of dissolution.

The members of what had once been an army—Napoleon himself and all his soldiers—fled without knowing whither, each concerned only to make his escape as quickly as possible from this position, of the hopelessness of which they were all more or less vaguely conscious.

So it came about that at the council at Málo-Yaroslávets, when the generals pretending to confer together expressed various opinions, all mouths were closed by the opinion uttered by the simple-minded soldier Mouton who, speaking last, said what they all felt: that the one thing needful was to get away as quickly as possible; and no one, not even Napoleon, could say anything against that truth which they all recognized.

But though they all realized that it was necessary to get away, there still remained a feeling of shame at admitting that they must flee. An external shock was needed to overcome that shame, and this shock came in due time. It was what the French called *"le hourra de l'Empereur."*

The day after the council at Málo-Yaroslávets Napoleon rode out early in the morning amid the lines of his army with his suite of marshals and an escort, on the pretext of inspecting the army and the scene of the previous and of the impending battle. Some Cossacks on the prowl for booty fell in with the Emperor and very nearly captured him. If the Cossacks did not capture Napoleon then, what saved him was the very thing that was destroying the French army, the booty on which the Cossacks fell. Here as at Tarútino they went after plunder, leaving the men. Disregarding Napoleon they rushed after the plunder and Napoleon managed to escape.

When *les enfants du Don* might so easily have taken the Emperor himself in the midst of his army, it was clear that there was nothing for it but to fly as fast as possible along the nearest, familiar road. Napoleon with his forty-year-old stomach understood that hint, not feeling his former agility and boldness, and under the influence of the fright the Cossacks had given him he at once agreed with Mouton and issued orders—as the historians tell us—to retreat by the Smolénsk road.

That Napoleon agreed with Mouton, and that the army retreated, does not prove that Napoleon caused it to retreat, but that the forces which influenced the whole army and directed it along the Mozháysk (that is, the Smolénsk) road acted simultaneously on him also.

CHAPTER XIX

A man in motion always devises an aim for that motion. To be able to go a thousand miles he must imagine that something good awaits him at the end of those thousand miles. One must have the prospect of a promised land to have the strength to move.

The promised land for the French during their advance had been Moscow, during their retreat it was their native land. But that native land was too far off, and for a man going a thousand miles it is absolutely necessary to set aside his final goal and to say to himself: "Today I shall get to a place twenty-five miles off where I shall rest and spend the night," and during the first day's journey that resting place eclipses his ultimate goal and attracts all his hopes and desires. And the impulses felt by a single person are always magnified in a crowd.

For the French retreating along the old Smolénsk road, the final goal—their native land—was too remote, and their immediate goal was Smolénsk, toward which all their desires and hopes, enormously intensified in the mass, urged them on. It was not that they knew that much food and fresh troops awaited them in Smolénsk, nor that they were told so (on the contrary their superior officers, and Napoleon himself, knew that provisions were scarce there), but because this alone could give them strength to move on and endure their present privations. So both those who knew and those who did not know deceived themselves, and pushed on to Smolénsk as to a promised land.

Coming out onto the highroad the French fled with surprising energy and unheard-of rapidity toward the goal they had fixed on.

Besides the common impulse which bound the whole crowd of French into one mass and supplied them with a certain energy, there was another cause binding them together—their great numbers. As with the physical law of gravity, their enormous mass drew the individual human atoms to itself. In their hundreds of thousands they moved like a whole nation.

Each of them desired nothing more than to give himself up as a prisoner to escape from all this horror and misery; but on the one hand the force of this common attraction to Smolénsk, their goal, drew each of them in the same direction; on the other hand an army corps could not surrender to a company, and though the French availed themselves of every convenient opportunity to detach themselves and to surrender on the slightest decent pretext, such pretexts did not always occur. Their very numbers and their crowded and swift movement deprived them of that possibility and rendered it not only difficult but impossible for the Russians to stop this movement, to which the French were directing all their energies. Beyond a certain limit no mechanical disruption of the body could hasten the process of decomposition.

A lump of snow cannot be melted instantaneously. There is a certain limit of time in less than which no amount of heat can melt the snow. On the contrary the greater the heat the more solidified the remaining snow becomes.

Of the Russian commanders Kutúzov alone understood this. When the flight of the French army along the Smolénsk road became well defined, what Konovnítsyn had foreseen on the night of the eleventh of October began to occur. The superior officers all wanted to distinguish themselves, to cut off, to seize, to capture, and to overthrow the French, and all clamored for action.

Kutúzov alone used all his power (and such power is very limited in the case of any commander in chief) to prevent an attack.

He could not tell them what we say now: "Why fight, why block the road, losing our own men and inhumanly slaughtering unfortunate wretches? What is the use of that, when a third of their army has melted away on the road from Moscow to Vyázma without any battle?" But drawing from his aged wisdom what they could understand, he told them of the golden bridge, and they laughed at and slandered him, flinging themselves on, rending and exulting over the dying beast.

Ermólov, Milorádovich, Plátov, and others in proximity to the French near Vyázma could not resist their desire to cut off and break up two French corps, and by way of reporting their intention to Kutúzov they sent him a blank sheet of paper in an envelope.

And try as Kutúzov might to restrain the troops, our men attacked, trying to bar the road. Infantry regiments, we are told, advanced to the attack with music and with drums beating, and killed and lost thousands of men.

But they did not cut off or overthrow anybody and the French army, closing up more firmly at the danger, continued, while steadily melting away, to pursue its fatal path to Smolénsk.